W9-BGQ-682

For Claudio A.

Copyright © 2004 by NordSüd Verlag AG, Gossau Zürich, Switzerland
First published in Switzerland under the title *Dodos Zirkus-Abenteuer*.
English translation copyright © 2005 by North-South Books Inc., New York

All rights reserved. No part of this book may be reproduced or utilized in any form or by any means,
electronic or mechanical, including photocopying, recording, or any information storage and
retrieval system, without permission in writing from the publisher.

First published in the United States, Great Britain, Canada, Australia, and New Zealand in 2005
by North-South Books, an imprint of NordSüd Verlag AG, Gossau Zürich, Switzerland.
Distributed in the United States by North-South Books Inc., New York.

Library of Congress Cataloging-in-Publication Data is available.
A CIP catalogue record for this book is available from The British Library.
ISBN 0-7358-1959-9 (TRADE EDITION)
1 3 5 7 9 HC 10 8 6 4 2
ISBN 0-7358-1960-2 (LIBRARY EDITION)
1 3 5 7 9 LE 10 8 6 4 2
Printed in Belgium

For more information about our books, and the authors and artists
who create them, visit our web site: www.northsouth.com

Serena Romanelli

Little Bobo's
Circus Adventure

ILLUSTRATED BY
Hans de Beer

NORTH-SOUTH BOOKS
NEW YORK / LONDON

Bobo the little orangutan lived in the lush tropical rain forest. He loved swinging through the jungle from tree to tree, but what he loved most was playing his violin at his special place by the river.

One day, while he was happily making beautiful music, he heard someone screaming.

A little dog was floating in the river, clinging to a log.

Oh, dear! thought Bobo. That dog is headed right for the waterfall! "I'm coming! Hold on!" cried Bobo, swinging himself across the river as fast as the wind.

Bobo managed to pull the dog out of the water just in the nick of time.

"Oh, thank you!" said the dog, panting. "You saved me! What is your name?"

"I'm Bobo, an orangutan."

"And I'm Tosca," she answered, shaking the water out of her fur and splashing Bobo from head to toe.

"How did you get here?" asked Bobo.

"I ran away. I couldn't stand it any more," explained Tosca. "I ran and ran and then I slipped and fell into the river. And then you saved me!"

"Why did you run away?" Bobo asked.

"I was very unhappy at the circus," explained Tosca. "There was a cockatoo there who was so jealous of my singing that he made my life miserable."

"Well, you're safe now," Bobo said, giving the dog a reassuring pat.

Bobo looked down at his violin bow. "Oh, no!" he cried. "It's broken! I'll never play again!"

"I'm very sorry, Bobo," said Tosca. "But . . . wait! These strings are horsehair. I know where we can find some! Come on, Bobo!"

Together they headed upstream. Bobo proudly pointed out the sights along the way. Tosca was thrilled by everything she saw.

"Oh, Bobo," she said. "I never knew the jungle was so wonderful!"

"Bobo," said Tosca, "once your bow is fixed, we can perform together. You can play and I'll sing. Listen." Tosca started to sing. Her voice was so shrill it gave Bobo goose bumps.

"Astonishing!" he said kindly.

By afternoon they had reached the edge of the rain forest. There stood a gaily striped circus tent. Now it was Bobo's turn to be thrilled. He stared in wonder at the sight.

"When we've found the horsehair, will you take me back to the jungle with you?" asked Tosca.

"Why not!" said Bobo with a smile. "There is room in the jungle for everyone!"

When it got dark they sneaked down to the circus. Bobo was a bit frightened, but when he heard the circus music he crept closer and closer until he found an opening in the tent. Curious, he peered inside.

"No! Wait! Don't do that!" cried Tosca. "They'll see you!" Then she whispered, "Come, I'll show you a safer place."

Tosca led Bobo under the stage. From there he watched in amazement—dazzled by the bright lights and the circus band. Suddenly there was silence, then a drum solo as the chimpanzee twins entered the ring. Bobo watched them play together on a single cello. It was such a thrilling performance that he didn't even notice the singing cockatoo!

After the show Tosca led Bobo to the circus ponies. "Don't be scared," she told him. "They are very small ponies." Tosca explained everything to the ponies, who were glad to give Bobo a few strands of hair from their tails.

"Just don't pull it out, please," they said and showed Bobo where to find scissors.

"Thank you so much!" said Bobo, carefully placing the horsehair in his violin case. "Why don't you come with us to the jungle?" he asked.

But the ponies refused. They preferred an open meadow where they could gallop.

Bobo turned to Tosca. "I'd really like to meet your friends, the chimpanzee twins," he said.

"Isa and Bella? Of course!" replied Tosca. "We have to be careful though. They live right next to the mean cockatoo. If he discovers I'm back, he'll call for the owners to lock me up. He's so jealous of my singing."

Bobo and Tosca crept through the circus wagons, not making a sound.

The twins greeted Tosca with great excitement. "We're so glad you are back again!" they chattered.

"I won't be staying," said Tosca. "This is my friend Bobo. He saved my life and he's taking me back to the jungle with him."

"The jungle? Really? Can we come with you?" asked the twins.

"Of course," said Bobo. "There's room in the jungle for everyone!"

As they packed their things they noticed Bobo's violin case.

"Oh, look! A little cello!" said Isa.

"Can you play it all by yourself?" asked Bella.

"Oh, yes," said Bobo. "I play like this."

Bobo grabbed his violin bow and waved it in the air. *Crash!* He knocked over a pile of juice cans.

"Oh no!" wailed Tosca, as the cockatoo came flying in, wings flapping angrily.

"So you're back again," said the cockatoo gruffly. "Just wait until I alert the owners. They'll put you in chains forever! Ha, ha!" He took a deep breath, all ready to sound the alarm, but Bobo quickly grabbed his beak and held it shut.

"Shh!" warned Bobo. "Don't tell on Tosca. I have a much better idea. Why don't you join us in the jungle? You could sing all day and all night and have flying races with the other cockatoos."

The cockatoo lowered his head and suddenly burst into tears. "Cockatoos in the jungle?" he asked incredulously.

"Ever since I was captured, I haven't sat in a tree or talked to another bird. I'm so unlucky." The cockatoo sobbed and sobbed. "Oh, I am so very unhappy!"

"Don't worry!" said Tosca kindly. "Once you're in the jungle, you will be happy again. Come on, let's go!"

"To the jungle! To the jungle!" cried the twins.

"To the jungle!" cried the cockatoo.

Now they all live happily in the tropical rain forest. Bobo's violin bow is as good as new. And his jungle band is bigger and better, with the chimpanzee twins on their cello and Tosca, the cockatoo, and his new girlfriend singing along.

But early in the morning Bobo loves to sit alone on the rock by the river, playing his special serenades. The music is beautiful and it's as if the whole rain forest is listening to him.